Neon Hemlock Press
www.neonhemlock.com
@neonhemlock

And What Can We Offer You Tonight
Premee Mohamed

Cover Illustration by Carly Allen-Fletcher
Cover Design by dave ring

Interior Bicchieri Illustration by Kat Weaver

Paperback ISBN-13: 978-1-952086-25-0
Ebook ISBN-13: 978-1-952086-26-7

Premee Mohamed
AND WHAT CAN WE OFFER YOU TONIGHT

Neon Hemlock Press

THE 2021 NEON HEMLOCK NOVELLA SERIES

NEON HEMLOCK

And What Can We Offer You Tonight

BY PREMEE MOHAMED

This story is dedicated to the ones who cannot be explained.

Bicchieri

HONOUR   GLAMOUR   SPLENDOUR

One

The dead girl woke and asked for her perfume and we gave it to her and she slept again.

And when she did so I felt glad I had not let anyone rifle through her things as often happened before the funeral. Someone might have been wearing her scent at the ceremony but no one was.

So now she lies on my bed with her bluewhite hand curled around the glowing vial. The one thing she wanted.

Nero sniffs, leans a shoulder gingerly against the doorway, avoiding his newly-implanted wings. "They do that with dinoflagellates, you know. It's nothing special."

"Don't be jealous," I tell him. Of course he cannot help it, he is very young, and anyway we are all of us a little rattled right now, I would say that none of us are really acting like ourselves, not *really*.

Someone needs to tell, someone whispers just outside the cracked door of my room, and someone whispers back *Shhh! What is wrong with you?* and someone else adds *What the* fuck *is wrong with you?*

For now I think the secret is safe. But the owners of our House will find out at some point. Not from me and not from my fellow courtesans, and need has nothing to do with what we do anyway. Does it. Ever. Has it. Ever.

Nero gets up to stand watch in the hallway and that leaves me in here with the dead girl who is not dead.

Two

This morning we crept out to the abandoned church, a dignified flotilla, ten and twenty and thirty and at the last perhaps forty boats bobbing in the dark with our red lanterns, and for a moment it was pretty and calm, Nero smiling for the first time in days, balancing lightly in the prow and holding up his light like a statue, and *Sit down, sit down, fool*, the hisses from the back, the others disliking the rocking on the flat oily water, and then the church loomed ahead, a grand jagged ruin bleeding rust into the slowlapping sea.

We made mooring on silken ribbons and entrusted the boats to the god of the beautiful dead. The steps have been vanishing year by year but we still splashed up the last few and passed through the great doors and down the aisle, the coffin already waiting on the altar. And inside some of us walked and some of us paddled, not thrashing or kicking overmuch, so that the sound of the sea could enter also.

Our church has been our church for generations. No one knows how it all began: this dark procession, the laying out of the body. It occurred to me that these things—to prepare the dead, to gather in the act of mourning—are among the hardest to shift in a people. That they move slowly and stubbornly, and that people cling to the practices they know for centuries, millennia, through famine, war, assimilation, invasion, colonization, plague, decline, despair.

What cataclysm drove us to this broken place? Was it whole then? I feel certain it wasn't. Our rituals are too set in stone.

Cemeteries in the city have been mostly built over, the standard practice and the standard process: leveling, compaction, low areas filled with waste, high areas brought low. The few left are guarded like prisons, and only for the use of the very rich.

No one says anything about that, no one ordinary, everyone just puts their dead into a canal. Lots of those around. Free, too. Once, I know, there was an idea of eternal life, or life after death, but everyone has abandoned that idea except them, the rich I mean, who are like another species.

We have not even given our god a name. Maybe in another thousand years.

On the thick particleboard of the coffin we placed flowers, and on the damp and crawling walls we hung the necessary artifacts, each giving as tradition specified: something about the deceased, but also something of ourselves. A single earring, rendering its mate back at the house useless; one glove; a painting or a scrap of sheetmusic; a lock of hair; a prized lipstick. To represent her finest skills, those of which she was most proud, some illustrated the walls in grease-pencil, or tacked up the packaging of toys or whips, hoarded specially for memorials and set aside for these days.

And the priest did not bid us be quiet, because we are told to be quiet often enough. And he also gave us no name for that reason, because it is only in mourning that we use the names we like instead of the names we were given when we were purchased. Each part of the ritual has a purpose and each successful step has a consequence for the dead. So for duty's sake we played the game as it was necessary to be played and the priest blessed the final piece and placed it on the flat glossy lid of the coffin.

It was nearly sunrise, the funerals always happen at sunrise, that too is our tradition. Someone once said: *Yes, now, when we are set free, like fairies in a story, from our bondage, and fly the wide woods...*

but that itself is a fairy story. We are still bound. This place is the only one we can visit, and the owners of the House look away from our transgression like they look away from death, and the sky is blueblack as a bruise and the water is the same and between them, very often, is a single knife-thin slice of gold sun more beautiful than any metal and any gem at House of Bicchieri and more beautiful than any of us and more beautiful than any of our clients.

And one of the new girls was crying and disoriented, she had been sick on the boat; and luckily her dress was still clean, because we must present ourselves in the church as clean and proud. But she said, *This isn't how funerals go, this isn't how they go,* and someone questioned her, and was stunned to discover that she had attended one as a little girl; and I too was stunned. Till I began at the House I had never heard of a funeral. I repeat: you paid your respects to the family and you gave a few credits if you had them, and then the body was weighted and sunk in the closest canal.

Instead this girl crying, saying this was not what she remembered. Her family must have been wealthy. I wondered how she had come to the House. Not something we ever ask, that's the rule; that information is only offered freely, and only to friends. For you don't climb to us. You fall only, you don't climb. She had fallen, or been thrown. Now she would never rise again. A long sad time, never.

Someone comforted her, and we clambered upon the rounded backs of the pews to begin the last of the rites. Someone passed around a bag of sweets. Someone passed around a flask of liquor. Wrists rose pale in the darkness and were blessed with a dab of scent. We were defiant, we were dressed for no client, scented for no client, we had lit up our implants and fed our hair for no client. Only to honour the dead girl, who we all loved.

And the priest said, *Blessed are the bodies,* and we said, *Whose bodies.* And he said, *Yours. Yours.* And the girl who had been crying looked up all surprised and dried her face and recomposed herself.

Good girl. You fell far, I wanted to tell her, but you have fallen into our arms, and we will carry you as best we can. Hence this secret ceremony, hence the priest we pay from our own earnings, hence the boats, the finery, the coffin itself. The House will not let us have this and the city will not let us have this but have this we must for those very reasons.

In the distance small red lights, looping regular patterns like the flight of a moth, a govvy cull in the Lows. Popular neighbourhood for it. They can get their quota in a day or two, and laze around the rest of the month. A curse upon their name, a pox upon them, we could not be touched by a cull, the House made us safe, but all of us had left someone behind. May they sicken and die. May they go unremembered.

And the priest said, *This, your friend Winfield*, and at hearing her name she stirred and sat up and pushed open the coffin and flowers spilled off her like water, roses, jasmine, lilies, honeysuckle, and the ugly rip they had made to fake an 'autopsy' tore open its lazy stitches and filled with blossoms.

No one screamed but we are trained to control our screams and in looking back actually I was very proud at our silence, which was stunned but absolute.

And she tried to get out of the coffin but could not. The priest fainted. We climbed from the pews and propped him up out of the water and took her home.

Three

G ive her to me, I said then, and because I have been in the House for so long, because I am nearly thirty years old, they obeyed me. Or obeyed my seniority at any rate. Before the ceremony I hissed and whisked people away from her room; now I probably will not need to. Even those who did not attend and do not know what to fear will have the vague knowledge that if the road to mortality runs two ways now, that if she is not alive, and she is not dead, her room is certainly filled with numinous spirits.

I asked for her without a plan in mind but we'd better do *something*. Demand is high to get in the House of Bicchieri, maybe the highest in all of the city, and the owners will not let the room languish without an occupant for long; it's not making a profit while it's empty of a warm and willing body.

I leave Winfield on top of the silkstitched duvet, hoping she is comfortable (hoping she will die again and solve this) and speak softly to such as I think I can trust, and they agree to pack up her things, conceal them piecemeal in their rooms, and safeguard them till we know what we are dealing with here.

No one says: But what *are* we dealing with? The answer is too terrible.

A girl who was dead, and then was not. A girl who was

dead in a fridge for a week, and was torn open, and finally, grudgingly surrendered to us for our rites. The owners threw us the 'autopsy' as a sop, because we complained, and because, they said, it would stop the whining...like scraps to a pack of dogs.

Fake, I thought then, and now I know for sure. They never did an autopsy. They didn't hire a medical examiner. Just ripped her open themselves, maybe with a steakknife from the kitchen. Forged the death certificate and sent it to the city. We could not protest, not without evidence. But the evidence is on my bed.

Awake again, Winfield touches the incision gingerly, its edges the colour of her low-cut gown. Her flesh shimmers like an opal and for a moment I think we should not have buried her in it, although I suppose we could not have known she would end up resembling it, like a chameleon, like a cuttlefish, that same bluish-silver fabric. There is no blood, not a drop. She says, "Jewel, is that you? You're all aglow."

"It's me, and I'm not. There's something wrong with your eyes, my lovely. Among other things."

"I died," she says. "He killed me."

"Who?"

"I don't remember."

Well.

Well. Well. We all thought as much, but I am struck with a sick full-body thud all the same. The way you hate to hear that you are right about an abomination. I take her hand, and eventually Nero comes back in and she takes his hand too, though he squirms, and she tells us that she was dead, but is no longer dead, and none of it makes sense, none, and we are asked to accept it and we do, because she is calm.

She tells us that she flew through a strange version of our city-state which floated on a maze of salt sand, not water; that something spoke to her and gave her life back, though not instructions. That she was in a place of instruction, not of apotheosis, not of prophecy; a sanctuary not because it was safe but because it was sacred. And she awoke in the sea-rotted cathedral and she knew it from other funerals and she looked for us and we were there.

"We'd never leave you," I tell her.

Nero says, "I'd rob you, but I'd never leave you."

Her first real smile. Winsome Winfield, who commanded
the highest prices in the entire House, who got to keep that
crucial five percent bonus from every client because of it, who
was actually allowed to receive tips, spreading them among us
with unthinking largesse, her wrist always buzzing with a new
name on her waitlist, lunging and scuffling for cancellations like
the suitors of Penelope...Winfield who had been here only two
years and was not considered 'used up,' though the owners never
said that about us, and they never called us whores or escorts or
hookers or sluts, always courtesans, because we were in a house,
a capital-H House.

In a House you are safe, even pampered. You have healthcare.
Three squares a day. Clean air. Your own room. Security
cameras. You might have a career of twenty or thirty years if you
are lucky and fit and diligent and obedient.

Or this might happen. Something like this. As had happened
a few times before.

"*Did* you rob me?" she says, and Nero looks at her solemnly,
How could you think that of me, and he says, "Only your earrings."

"Give them back, darling."

"But you—" he begins, and I nearly kick him before he stops
on his own, cheeks reddening under the golden-brown skin, the
dyed-fire brows. His ears positively glow. *But you won't need them
now*, he wants to say, *because you are dead.*

I want to say *What will you do now?* Which isn't much better
and I am so bad at this, I am so bad at saying the needed things,
the obvious things. She cannot work here, and you have to
work to live; no one else can look after you, because no one else
has anything any more. There's no such thing as a mutual-aid
society like in the old days when welfare stopped, there's no aid
now, no one has anything to give. Just mutuality without the
actual exchange of money or goods. The city is like the canals
which keep it alive: filled with garbage and killers, a terrible
silent deadly striving beneath the surface, regularly dredged, its
leavings crushed and processed for value, then discarded.

Had we not all seen, growing up, cull after cull after cull,
had we not taken in with infant ears that if you didn't have the

chip saying you were a worker, if your employer did not verify it, you were fair game, you had less value than a rat (for there are bounties on the rats now, both North and South halves of the city decreed it last year, ten credits for a tail), you only have value here, somewhere *like* here I mean, and I can say none of this.

No one says: My God, what are we going to *do* with you.

She cannot stay here, it is an impossibility. The waiting list to get into the House of Bicchieri is miles deep, no, an ocean abyss, you could wedge a mountain into it and watch it simply sink down into the darkness forever. In hours—because they know how long our ceremonies take—her room will be rearranged, sanitized, depersonalized, and reassigned. Tomorrow, or perhaps the day after tomorrow at the latest. She has nowhere to hide.

For us to reveal to the owners that she is not dead might simply mean they kill her again: for not being dead enough, staying dead enough, for what she knows and has seen, for what they did.

So she exists in this space where she cannot exist and cannot be allowed to exist. Not by any of us.

In a few hours, the clocks will strike and our appointments will begin and there is just nowhere to put her and for a second I feel a wild rush of despair that stings my eyes like a splash of canal water illuminated for a second by a sign: bright, chemical burn, replaced with darkness, why couldn't she just be dead, why, we mourned her, we performed the necessary acts, our secret rites that belong only to us, we risk our lives to properly look after the dead, and now she is back, and she has ruined everything, why couldn't she just decently die, we *cried* for her.

And I can feel Nero's thoughts drumming on the back of my neck, Nero who loved her, who loves everybody (he cannot help it, he was bought so young), who is a little mad with despair right now too. Finally, he says, "Maybe the roof?" and I think for a minute, maybe, it's not unused but it's not frequently used, being less prettified and landscaped and manicured than the rest of the place, of course there are some clients who like that, but she will not be found, I think, by management at any rate. It could be a temporary refuge.

I put her perfume into a pocket of her dress and lace it up

again where she has opened it seeking her bloodless lie of a wound. "Up we get," I say, "uppy-up," and Nero and I drag her down miles of silent hallway to the great gilt elevator. A shadow, at the end of the hallway? Someone fleeing? No, just an optical illusion, caused by the double mirrors I think. We are all paranoid even though we are all on the same side.

She lolls against us as the elevator clanks and jerks upwards, the noise an affectation, like so much else here (the stupid gazebos, the pergolas, the marble fauns that I hate, the benches poised coyly behind the loathsome topiaries, the picturesque fields of poppies and lavender against the ruthlessly sprayed, clipped, combed, compacted, dyed, and soundproofed turf).

The decorative brass grid of the cage leaves marks of fern and seashell on her bare, bluish arms. I imagine the three of us from behind like a court portrait rendered in oils: the three heads leaning together, the gold and the silver and the black. In life we are paid to imitate art.

On the roof we are struck with the wind, warm and humid, and the smell of the city: rotten, curiously chemical though, like a mouldy battery rather than mouldy food. The sky is indigo and the buildings below us are the same and the canals and the sea some miles away are the same and it is like being caught and tumbled in a great monotonous wave there in the wind with no walls around us and the hard golden light of the sunrise that was supposed to arrive as the priest finished the speech is here now, flung sideways and approaching with startling speed, amidst the small fiery lights of factories, boats, homes, and the glow-backed fish that live far below and sometimes rise just before dawn to lip the surface of the viscous water.

Winfield holds us in the noise and the openness of the wind and Nero and I put our arms around her waist, she feels light, emptied out, how could they, and I begin to say, *What will you do?* and she says, "I am going to kill him."

And the wind rips her words away and carries them around us and I picture them like small furious birds of prey, their talons piercing something furry and struggling.

Nero has the good sense to keep silent for once. I too say nothing. We watch the sun come up and then embrace her and return to work, taking the stairs down, tapping our wristbands against the clock, we are paid by the hour as well as per client, this is a good House, not like the others, we will always be safe, always looked after, and I think: When we go back up there she will be dead again. Not: When we go back up there she will be gone.

Four

But after our shift ends, of course, she is gone.

"Oh, bleeding Christ." My hands leap to my mouth. I picture only the wind picking her up, light as she is, using her expensive opal-coloured gown as a sail, we always bury the dead in their best, their very best, carrying her away in her best.

Then I shake my head, and practicality descends. She's young and she's pretty and she's dead but she's not a fool; she will have hidden someplace, and because the security system is largely infrared based to keep out vermin of various species and credit ratings, she can likely come and go at leisure. She is scheming, planning, to enact her revenge; she's good at this, savvy, she sees technology as toys.

Hiding. Spying. Trying to fill in that gap in her memory... the owners will have records, it is part of the understanding they make with our clients: phone numbers, addresses, maybe more. Or will Winfield find her enemy some other way? Is she beloved of a god now, will the god help a favourite out, like in the stories? Possessed by sharp-eyed Apollo, and sending out silver arrows. Possessed by owl-eyed Athene, and swinging your sword with such force and speed as would kill Ares himself. Or someone possessed by him. Why do I keep thinking about possession? The gods don't need our bodies.

"Do you know who it was?" Nero says, as we huddle out of the wind and pass a stik back and forth (unflavoured, unscented, the only kind we are allowed).

"No," I tell him. "But I can guess."

"Me too."

There is a slate, a menu of options...not many. Which tells you something too. The clients are sometimes permitted, for an extra fee, to take us off the property, for meals or 'cultural events' only, such as humiliating an ex-wife, and so I have seen the full range of restaurants the North city has to offer (we cannot cross the river), and I know the more expensive the establishment, the smaller their menu, and the most expensive ones have none at all, you eat what they give you. Someone else picks. You don't pick.

So we know this is a small menu. It was a man, a wealthy man, even more so (I think) than our usual clients, whose net worth generally veers into the stratosphere anyway; we are not one of those Houses where any ordinary family (our own, say) could save up for a few months to gift someone a trip to visit the expensive whores. It would not be possible.

Even more rich, even more elite than usual. Hm. But perhaps something else too...the way it was hushed up so quickly, the way we heard through the whisper walls not even the faintest hint of reparations, settlement, to the House that we've previously seen for the accidental death of a worker while with a client.

Something else, something...I don't know. Politically connected, perhaps, or neo-nobility from somewhere else, or the heir of one of those big conglomerates, you know the ones. Big. Like they bought planets and suchlike, like *moons* belong to them, or their family. Someone the owners do not just pander to, like everyone else, but also fear.

Of the clients I have seen coming in and out of the House, perhaps just five or six fit the description...I shake my head. "We're not going to help her."

"No, of course not."

"We're not murderers."

"No, no." He hunches over and his golden curls flop into his eyes, sweet Nero whose real name he's never revealed, purchased as Ganymede two years ago but of course there are a thousand Ganymedes in the city, what a cliché, rechristened as soon as he'd stepped in the door (the back door; front is for clients only), *You don't want him*, the owners had sniffed, *mistaken for one of* those, and that's what it means to work here: we are precious, rarefied, you don't want to be confused for something *not* that. The disdain dripping from their words, so your shoes slip on it.

Because if you are confused for *one of those*, if you fuck up: back out you go. Back out there to the city, sink or swim. And if you don't swim, immediately and strongly and far, far faster than all the others thrown out with you, you're cull fodder. We still say: bird in a gilded cage. But better a cage than an oven.

I slide my arm around him, avoiding the warm healing tissue of his new implants, and I put every bit of authority into my voice that I can. "No. She's on her own. We're not like that." Because if you say it, it becomes true.

"Of course we're not." He empties the stik, sets it on the thick black gravel, presses down with his thumb till it crumbles. The wind will pick up the scraps. Safety first.

I stand, pull him up, look down automatically. Down there, the filth, the lights. Something nagging at me. "When we first got her. Someone outside the door said *We should tell.* Or something like that. *We need to tell.* You were closer to the door, did you hear that?"

He nods uncertainly. His eyes are golden rings, matching the glow of his hair. You could almost read by those eyes, they become so hot and bright when he is agitated.

"Who said it?"

"I don't know," he says. "You know how it's hard to tell. With whispers. But...do you think..."

"No. It's nothing to worry about. We're not like *that* either."

"All of us?"

"I don't know. I hope so."

Five

Back inside we eat and nap, work out, endure the weekly medical (brisk as always, unremarkable as always, the phlebutton the only good part, watching the little sphere fill with red), lounge in the library, cuddle in front of the viewscreens, cocoon in our rooms.

Two hours till my next client and I think I will read and nap again, we are always a little tired, it comes from the weird shift system and your body simply never gets used to the constant changes, but I open my door and the scent comes at me, she doesn't like citrus, says it smells too much like disinfectant, other fruits, herbs, fig, blackberry, sage I think, pine resin, like the trees along the Singing Walk.

Winfield says evenly, "Did you know that they had cameras in here?"

I shut the door and press my thumb to the lock. "They're fakes. To make the clients behave. You know that."

"They're not. As it turns out. So now you know too."

I turn instinctively, though of course that's the worst thing to do if she's right, and stare at mine: the round lens shiny and clean and fake, comprising the mouth of the jar held by the simpering gilt cherub in his nest of flowers above the door. For more than a decade I have been told it was fake. I pass a hand suspiciously in front of the lens. "Win."

"I deactivated it," she says. "Then erased the recordings. They'll have to buy new ones for a couple of rooms. You, Iris, Samira, Flyboy..."

"You know he hates that. How?"

She tosses her hair impatiently and I wait, cringing, for a clump to fall to the floor, she is dead after all, but nothing happens; and she looks radiant, not alive, something else, brimming with light. The light of vengeance, I think with a little twist of envy. The light of fury. In my aubergine-wallpapered room with its inkily figured ferns, the bloodred duvet, the sepia headboard and floors, she is the brightest thing.

She says, "I broke into the study. Serpentine's study."

Miss Serpentine, I almost say, then laugh. Of course she doesn't have to use honorifics of any kind for the owners now. "But what good... "

"They had all the recordings, exterior and interior. And it shows viewcount. So I knew I was the first one who had accessed it. Actually I don't think they watch them, mostly, on off-hours," she adds, her voice filled with bile. "Just with clients. Later."

"Lawsuit city," I murmur.

She snickers. "A whole city of lawsuits. Skyscrapers, arcologies of lawsuits. Floating colonies of lawsuits. Anyway, I'm sure they don't let a single image get off the grounds."

"But they had him."

"...They had him. With me."

My knees give and I collapse onto the bed next to her and instinctively, as we all often do here, we take each other's hands. Hers is cold and dry, but strong, and a strange irregular pulse beats in her wrist. But she is dead; no one could have been emptied out like her and not be dead.

I squeeze her hand. She squeezes back. What can I say to her? She has seen her death, she saw herself killed, that is what she meant by *With me*. What beats inside her? No, stop it. She saw herself killed. She will never forget that, not for a single moment of her renewed life. She sought out and watched her murder and she really means to do this, whatever this is.

"He held me down, he held his hand over my face," she

says. "Over my mouth and nose, till it was done. It was not an accident."

"He wouldn't have told them it was," I tell her when she has told me the name, and I am obscurely proud that he was on both my longlist and my shortlist. My ears are ringing. "Someone like Pederssen, he'd have *bragged* about it. He wouldn't be afraid of anything the owners could do to him. They would have been afraid of him."

"No."

"Of him not coming back. Of losing his business."

"Oh," she says flatly. "Maybe. Maybe."

"People like him," I say, "don't have scandals. They have amusing little diversions." Then I remember I am speaking of her murder, and fall silent. I have said hateful things today. "I'm sorry."

"Don't be. You're right."

There's a very simple food web here, I think. Predators, prey. Prey fights for its life, as she must have fought. And out there somewhere, mother, father, family, friends, not even aware that she was here or dead. In any other world we would call him a monster and do what you do to monsters, which is kill him; but because he is who he is, we protect and revere him, we fawn at his feet, we forgive him his rampaging and ravaging, we go so far as to maybe kill those who would kill him. Imagine Beowulf showing up only to discover the Danes protecting Grendel, guarding him while he eats their people.

Her voice is steely, distant. "All the same, proud as he is, he won't come back here for ages. But his life is an insult on this Earth. I won't wait. I'll hunt him down like a rat. Go into the city and make him bleed."

"Win, no. Let it go."

"Let it *go*?"

"All right, we've been dancing around this. But I'm going to say it." As I speak she pulls her hand from mine and places it in her lap, staring at the wall. Our heads are twinned in the great mercury mirror, expressions identical. "You came back. We don't know how. And I'm tempted to say we don't know why either, but what if *why* is to give you a second chance at life? To do something else, something...meaningful."

She snorts. I flush when I realize it, humiliated that line insinuated itself into my speech: something the owners, Serpentine and Jasper (they like mineral names, and are always changing them) say. Especially in the early days of each new purchase, when people are disoriented and empty, ready to be filled with their apparently inspirational talks, like pouring poison into a cup.

They say that we *are* doing meaningful work: that we are generating profit, not everybody can do that you know, that we are employable, not everybody is that you know. That we are providing company and comfort, listening ears, welcoming orifices, that we are using both body and mind to help others in this awful wreck of a city, that we are a small shining light of civilization as well as civility, that we are a torch held aloft the darkness and separate from it because of our intent to do good in the world...

I thought I had ignored those speeches. I certainly scoffed at them when they were given. Now I see they were grit and have become, inside me, a pearl. Misshapen, I suspect. Not nice and round. "You're a miracle. A medical miracle. Probably among other types...how many are there? But look, darling, you can't waste this chance. No one else has ever gotten it. You're absolutely unique in the history of the world and you're just going to...to get yourself killed again. Or worse."

"Worse?"

"Well, I don't know. Use your imagination. Like the movies." I watch us in the mirror, meeting her eyes. "Captured. Studied. Vivisected!"

"But nothing hurts now," she says dreamily, and stands, and trails a hand over my head. "How dare you tell me not to, Jewel. *Darling.* How dare you. Maybe this is precisely the reason I was brought back. Maybe a god asked me to come back and be the hand of justice. Maybe a god said: *Not everybody deserves to be alive. But you do. And he doesn't.* Hmm?"

I stare up at her, the clinging dabs of perfume glowing behind her ear. How we had loved her when she came, I thought. Instantly, unstintingly, and because of this: because she said the things we thought in our worst nights, the things we whispered through gritted teeth into the pillows, she was like a cold clean air blowing through the dust and fug and musk of the House. She was the only person who seemed unafraid.

"Pederssen can try to unmake me," she says. "But he cannot unperson me. I will always be who I am. And you will always be who you are. A coward, huddling in this House with her safe little job, afraid of the city. Afraid of what I might bring to you from it. Contaminating this place. That's what you're worried about. Isn't it?"

"I'm worried *for* you. You've already risked enough, breaking into the study, doing what you did. You'll be caught."

"Liar. Look at you. You're worried about four square inches of skin. You're worried about the light on your wristband. I'm not afraid of the city."

"You should be. What neighbourhood were you from again? West Jovia? We used to call that Redlake. You know how bad it was. It's worse now. You've known it long enough to know what it can do."

"Survived it long enough. And will again." She smiles, as if I am forgiven. Now her teeth look like her dress and her skin: polished, iridescent. "I'll go. It seems there is no help to be found here."

"Winfield. Don't."

"I'll come tell you when I'm done," she says. "We can have a party."

"*Don't.* Think of the rest of us. If you..."

"I'll see you later, Jewel."

When she leaves, I get the sense (fleeting, inevitable) that a safe-box has just been emptied of its contents; I feel robbed.

For days I read the news with a certain horror, the horror of anticipation, as if earthquakes or hurricanes had been predicted, and I suppose it is almost the same thing, it is the same feeling because it is the same thing: What will she bring upon us if she does what she says she will do? It would be like an earthquake.

Well, she'd better not, that's all I'm saying. She wouldn't do that to us, her friends, put us out on the street. (Briefly. *Briefly* out on the street. Then we will be off the street, and in a canal.)

But there's nothing, there's never anything, and I find I have to scour all the sections, we still get a newspaper, we are not allowed personal devices you can search, so even absent from us she is an inconvenience: his murder not on the front page? Perhaps an oversight. In the Business section, because of his family's business? No, not there. Books, perhaps? Why? Well, he wrote books, didn't he. He wrote those self-help books. Finance? What's the difference between Business and Finance? And so on.

"You're very up on current events these days," someone chirps behind me a week later at breakfast.

I turn: not someone I know—not new, I don't think, I've seen her a few times, but she works in the other wing where I don't often go, as you have to cross through the atrium where a girl hung herself eight years ago. She is young, sly-looking, pretty; her hair writhes slowly around her shoulders, its reticulated pattern like fall leaves. "Do you need the paper, darling?"

"I'd love the entertainment section if you're done with it."

I fish it out, hand it over. If my instincts have kept me alive this long, I think, I should obey them: and there is something a little off about her brittle brightness, something that is not the play-acting we often do. "Long way to walk for the comics, isn't it?"

"Oh, no no. Miss Serpentine and Mister Jasper reassigned me to the East wing. There was an empty room. So lovely to have a window."

"I quite agree."

Win's room. You, I think. You whispered in the hallway after the funeral. You, just a few feet from my door. Who corrected you? Who defended you? Are there *factions* now, in this place where our unity is the only thing we have ever counted on to stay alive? "And you can buy good little plants at Klaas for your windowsills," I add, referring to the House store in our wing, the only place we can spend our money. "They can order in plants from the city if you want something special...someone did show you where it was, didn't they?"

"No! I'd love a tour."

I refold the paper, meet her eyes for a moment: bright violet. A mod colour that was popular when I was a teenager. Comes with its own set of assumptions. "Well," I begin, and stop as I catch—not quite, my intuition catches, not my eyes, even my nose, the harsh smell of blood and nanofluids—the merest blink of the medical capsule traveling at its top speed through the transparent glass tube that runs along the ceiling of the Great Room, where clients rarely look.

The others glance up at the subsonic whine of eaten air, then snarl and flinch, protecting their breakfast or books, as I rush from the room, past the stranger, hiking up my skirts with both hands, till I am pressed against the tingling forcefield of the infirmary steriglass, ill with a different dread.

Seven

"No," Nero says, "it doesn't hurt, it's fine," and Miss Serpentine and Mister Jasper smile and coo over him, their investment, soon he'll be tuned-up and waxed to a high shine again, never you fear my dumpling, my honeycake, and I wait till they sweep from the room, favouring me with their most brilliant smiles, as matchy-matchy as surgery and injections and delicate layers of painterly cosmetics can make them, as brilliant as diamonds, and I lean over the railing of his bed. There is an awful stink of blood still, and disinfectant, harsh artificial lemon.

Nero weeps and hides his face with one hand and reaches for me with the other, groping the air till I take it and press it to my face. I will not ask him what happened; it is clear enough. The new wings on his back—the best, the most expensive, the most natural that can be made, the envy of any real bird in the sky— were ground zero of this attack.

One is bandaged and apparently intact, but the other is clearly broken, carefully splinted into a frame of small articulated metal and plastic pieces, like spiders protectively cradling the long white arc. His face too is battered, one eye puffed shut.

The wings are new, yes, but they are stunningly tough; they are crafted, feather by feather, out of the stuff once used in bulletproof vests. Someone did this on purpose. Someone held him down and did this. Someone put him facedown on the floor at some point and wrenched the wing open as he tried to protect it and then someone twisted till it bent and then broke.

No accident. Not even a pretense of an accident.

"My teeth are all right." He chuckles through his tears, gathering up the loose strands of his composure. "I think that's the important thing."

"Yes, you still have your million-dollar looks. You vain beast."

"I know."

"You peacock. But oh, your..." His dark, rosy face is ashen from pain. I want to weep too, it must hurt so badly, and they never give you enough drugs here, as if the threat of lying unmedicated after a beating would prevent the next one. We should be used to the world in which the victim is punished instead of the instigator but something inside us still cries out that it is wrong, not just logically wrong, causatively or chronologically wrong, but wrong in some other way as well. Something deeper. More cellular.

I kiss the palm of his hand, unharmed but bearing a teardrop-shaped splatter of blood. "Who was it?"

"What does it matter?"

"It might have been..." I hesitate. "Well, I don't want to say revenge. But a...a warning. Maybe. More than a slap on the wrist. Because you and I are the ones who...all right, listen, just now while I was eating breakfast—"

The window darkens, and we both draw away instinctively, startled more than actually frightened, and he yelps as the splint on his broken wing adjusts itself with an affronted little hydraulic whine.

Winfield slithers into the room with boneless ease, a joyful swing from the top frame belying her bared teeth, a filthy avenging angel in this spotless place, her bare feet squelching onto the tile floor. Her hair is lank, the opalescent lilac strands matted together like lace. She looks delighted with herself. "Tell me who did this."

"Thank *God* for this catheter," Nero says when he catches his breath.

"Who?" She leans over the hospital bed, grasping the railing. She no longer smells of perfume and the flowers of the grave, but the city: smoke, trash, fish, the clinging gloop of canals. "I'll have a word."

"Don't," I say. "We're all in deep enough, Nero. Someone is passing things to the owners, someone in the House, spying on us...you don't know what'll happen. Retaliation."

"You haven't done anything wrong," Win says, not looking at me. "Ignore her. Tell me."

He stares up at her for a long moment, half-defiant, a contrarian, now that he has been asked he certainly will not tell, he might have told us before, then seems to come to some kind of conclusion, you can almost hear him think, *Retaliation, you say?* and light flares green and gold behind his eyes. "Draavik."

Even in my anger I find myself unsurprised; he's slapped a few of us around. There is a lazy cruelty to him that no one doubted would become intentional, deliberate, to one of us, or perhaps to one of his wives back home, or his kids or his dog or his employees or maybe all of them. Whoever was within reach when he decided to stop toying about with his impulses and take off their muzzles.

Winfield straightens, meets my gaze. "I won't kill him," she says. "Princess. Look at you. Look at your face. No, I'll just teach him a lesson."

"First murder, now this? You've got to knock it off, Win. This won't get you any closer to Pederssen."

"I haven't done a murder," she says. "And this is just a friendly chat. Help him see the error of his ways."

I hesitate, chewing on my lip, and glance back over my shoulder to see if anyone is watching us through the steriglass. Little spy with her cheap purple eyes. Now I know of her existence, and now she must know I know. Good old predictable Jewel, reading the paper every morning, sitting in the same place, getting the same breakfast. Outwit her by zigging where she wants me to zag. Can I? I move in a straight line every day.

Win smiles, taking visible pleasure in my worry. "Help me. Come with me. See for yourself."

"See..."

"What it's like." She leans on the bed, her face nearly meeting mine. Bones are visible now beneath the shimmering fabric of her gown. "What I do now."

"What?"

"I send messages. I'm a poet, really." She glances up at the ceiling for a moment, pretending to compose something. "Come with me and send a sonnet to the rat you think is running around the House. Tell them: I'm not afraid of you. Tell them: I know what you're doing. Tell them: And there will be consequences for this. For Draavik. And for you."

Oh. Now that. *Would* be something. But.

I waver, still clinging to Nero's hand. His face is a sunrise: filled with impossible, malicious delight. At the thought of someone not just sticking up for him, I think, because we all do that when we can, but someone getting back at the bully. Bursting, if even for a second, that bubble of money and power and arrogance and invulnerability that surrounds them...and I feel it, I feel what he feels, as if it is being conducted through our skin, breathed in with the harsh stink of lemon. I feel it and I want it. I want to see it, at least. I want to see a moment's justice.

Draavik won't have gotten far, I think, that small practical voice inside me that I hate, that makes the others call me *Auntie* and *Grandma*. He would have spent how long in Serpentine and Jasper's office? Drinking gin with them and watching their hands flutter in apology, oh *no* had he perhaps damaged his fists on their thoughtless courtesan's face? Did that awful boy's blood stain your lovely suit? How can we make it better, Mr. Draavik?

God I hate him. I hate him.

Not justice, no. She won't mete out justice. But as close as we can get, because no one else is handing it out these days either, the so-called authorities are not for people like us except in the sense that we may sometimes be on the receiving end.

Nero smiles, seeing our faces, he is so good at that, the one who spent years reading people in a split second so he could stay alive. "Oh Win," he says sweetly, "I do abhor the use of violence."

"Well we won't tell you about it then," she says, pleased. "See if you can sleep. Work on your horrible novel. We'll be back before you know it."

"Bring some good drugs!"

Winfield smirks, and leaves the way she came in, swift and almost boneless, the flick of a snake.

When we are alone his face slams shut like a door. "God this is fucking nuts," he says. "Jewel, you're not really going out into the city with a zombie vigilante."

I look down at her dirty bare footprints on the floor, and smudge them carefully with my shoe. The cleaners will crawl around here soon enough and get the rest. "Don't say it like that."

"But you're *not* though. Not really."

"We'll be fine. And you, you heard nothing, you saw nothing. You were off your little curly-headed gourd on painkillers, and I was upset and went back to my room."

"Yes, yes you were. Needing a good cry at the death of beauty. Heartbroken at what happened to my face."

"Passive voice," I tell him as I leave. "Remember we said to watch for that. You hack."

"I'm going to write you into my book so I can kill you," he calls down the hallway.

"Yeah yeah."

Eight

I want to change before I join Winfield outside somewhere (but where? she didn't say, expecting me to know) but at the same time, I am seized for just a second with her madness or Nero's contrarianism, *why*, goddammit, why, if she is swanning about the place in her expensive finery, can I not do the same? Well, lots of reasons, good ones, not least that I don't have anything but expensive finery in my wardrobe, but I don't care. In my crimson gown flecked with golden ferns I go, and I tell myself that even though the colour of the silk is as loud as a shout, my passage will be entirely unheard.

Where did the spy go? I wish I knew her name. At any rate I don't spot her as I slink swiftly through the House, trying to look both distraught and busy, though of course that doesn't mean she's not around, and slip into the Long Promenade and through the door that leads down and then over and then out into the hangar, a strange great dim high-ceilinged cavern which seems to be moving restlessly all over its surface like the skin of an animal shivering in its sleep, an illusion created by dozens of gray-suited mechanics and laborers and dozens more gray-enamelled cleaners labouring along on their little treads keeping the dust off the gleaming craft, polishing even the struts of the roof.

No one looks up as I pass. We aren't forbidden from the hangar, no one can fly anything here anyway, and we've all visited now and again with a client; a stray courtesan here or there doesn't attract attention. Its main appeal is that it has a small exterior door leading to one of the lawns which the mowers use and which therefore is left unlocked on the inside, and I take this, casually, and shut it behind me with a discreet click.

The world is too big. I have been inside too long. This is not like the roof, bounded by its neat white stucco, making us safe up to chest-height, this is like...a sky, a mile of grass on either side, the trees too tall, a hopping thing that startles me for a second: a crow furricking in the turf. God what have I done, I turn and the door is locked of course, I turn back and Winfield steps out from behind one of the trembling cedars, smiling, twigs in her hair like a dryad. "I knew you'd come this way. Did anyone see you?"

"I don't think so."

"Tell me about this spy."

I talk as we go, my voice wavery, and I hate this tremolo, it shames me. Why can I not be as brave and careless as her? (Because I am alive, because I am still alive.)

The sky is slaty and still and dull, punctured by occasional agonizing stabs of light. As we head towards the wall separating us from the city I glance back at the House: a stacked white monstrosity, artfully stained to appear mottled with age rather than pollution; the saccharine prettiness of its lawns; the white-gravel path to the elaborate, insectile front doors; the bare-breasted and bare-bottomed statues littering the place; the self conscious placement of each tree and flower. My home.

Some people, I think, some people pay so much money not even to take my clothes off and come against my thigh, but just to be here, physically here, just to breathe a moment's clean air, smell the chlorophyll.

And for a second I ache for it, to just turn and go back, I feel love, what feels like genuine love, for the white walls, the golden lights, knowing my little room is up there, a sanctuary with a lock on the door to keep out the monsters, and it overpowers my anger and it overpowers my glee and I smell something sour and terrible: fear coming out of my pores, the broken-down molecules of it, the acrid metabolites of it, so that a dog could nose me a mile away.

I say nothing, do nothing, follow Winfield's quick-moving back, the silvery silk stained and spattered like a map. I'm here now, and I must push down the fear for a little while at least to help her, if that is what I'm doing. See, I think in a vague way at the rest of the people in the House as it retreats behind us, see, I am not so old, I am not so hardened in my ways.

In fact I feel ten years old for a second. No, nine. The last year of adventures, because you become eligible for the cull at double-digits (your band goes dark that morning, you can be targeted, it's all legal, all above-board).

Nine, when you could still climb the rooftops, play pretend, form your little gangs and mobs, speak your secret language, leap and know that even a long fall could be survived, the way a spider can fall from a height. No going back from that birthday. And no going back from this. There's a gap in my schedule right now, it's true, and as such I won't be missed, but if I am late for the client that arrives at noon, that will be observed and reported. And there will be consequences.

Deal with that when it happens, I tell myself firmly. Be the sensible one later. For now, be someone else. You're always two things at once anyway. All of us are.

We find a gate in the wall, hidden behind a thick wall of ivy that shades, as designed, from black at the top through violet, red, pink, orange near where it brushes the grass. With insulting ease Win reaches through the pink and punches in a passcode and we are through, and I don't need to ask whether she has busted or zapped the exterior cameras, she moves with such confidence, as if she does this a dozen times a day.

The gate shut behind us, we trot down a long set of concrete steps slick with moss and lichen, I had forgotten how high the House was set above the city, and then we are at street level, and back in what used to be our home.

It has been long enough—let me think. Eight months? Ten? that I stop in my tracks and gape. Winfield pauses patiently while I do this, so that we do not get separated. Safety in

numbers. Survival, really. I wonder if she felt like this too that
first morning, sneaking out and back here.

The city, the city. I forgot all this so quickly, my mind let
it evaporate...no. It was not a passive thing. I pushed it down
on purpose, but kept it all. As real and solid and vivid as this,
something you could touch and smell, all of these details—the
signs, the snarled ivy and thorned weeds, the rat shit, broken-
down buildings, trashcan fires, tilting streetlights, the city doesn't
look after any of these people, the city doesn't *want* to look after
them or even itself because it does not see itself as a home, not a
workplace either, just where people happen to be, temporarily,
making money for people who live elsewhere. Because there is
nowhere else to live now but a city. Because there is nothing but
cities. But in the House, you are supposed to forget about the
city.

"It hasn't changed," Win says.

"No. Just us. It's all relative."

"All relative," she agrees.

We are surrounded by narrow streets and water of various
depths, and I spot one of the great strange armoured indigo-
coloured fish always waiting to suck down a little boat, the kids
sitting on the ledges and bollards keeping one eye on it as they
dangle their fishing lines in the thick water, a mudlark just down
the block from us oddly familiar, was she here when I lived here?
shuffling, eagle-eyed, with her long clawed tool probing into the
overflow gutters alongside the canals, something about her gait
I feel sure I know, and the last time, the last dozen times, I have
left the walls, it has been on the arm of a client, and I saw this
place, my old home, for just a split second between the wall and
the copter, the wall and the hover, the wall and the car, the wall
and (on at least one memorable occasion) the carriage.

"Don't freak out," Win says.

"I'm not."

"Uh huh."

My heart pounds. Can you die of this, can you die of
memory? I take Winfield's hand as she pulls us out of the shadow
of the wall, get it over with, people nodding to us interestedly, *It's
not often*, you can hear them think, *that the little decorative songbirds*

hop free from their cage there...look how fast they're walking, they must have been sent out for something very important.

"Up," she says ten or twelve blocks later, and we climb a ladder bolted to a crumbling brick building dotted in a thousand colours with the eager lichen that eats dirty air, and I feel like I am climbing into my childhood, climbing back digit by digit, job by job, and she laughs at my laughter as we surmount the roof and wind carefully between the beds of soil and plants protected by barbed wire. I remember these rooftop gardens and am secretly pleased that they have not changed; it is like seeing an old friend whose face lights up with recognition just as yours does.

The old woman in the little cinderblock watchtower at the far corner watches us cross but makes no move for her shotgun, swathed inside her tightly-wrapped tea-brown blanket, fringed tassels draped over the visible trigger. Winfield must have been here before, or maybe this is her headquarters now, and I suppose a dead-now-alive girl is no weirder than anything else you have seen if you are old enough here, and we're not a threat to the plants or to the shacks around them where people sleep.

We move to the very edge of the roof and Win removes a brick and takes out a pair of binoculars.

"I bought these in the market," she says, as it runs through its flickering, glitchy initialization. "One of a kind. Here we go." She presses a button on the side, and laughs as she peers through them. "Oh, it's too easy. It's too easy from up high. What's the saying? Is it shooting apples in a barrel?"

"Is it shooting *ducks* in a barrel?"

"I don't think so. Why would you put ducks in a barrel? Apples, at least, you can... here."

She hands me the heavy, sticky device and shows me how to focus the view. At first there is only chaos, a storm of different-coloured pixels. And then it fades to gray, and a small, dark-red clot of pixels marches confidently away from us, down the cross-street. "How did you—"

"Reprogrammed the infrared sensor to switch between heat mode and credit rating," she laughs. "It's unbearable. I had to recalibrate it a few times. Lot of hustlers out there with fake numbers."

I swing the binoculars down. In the slow stream of traffic you can see it, the artifice of Draavik's car, dinged-up with stick-on rust, dents, scratches, entire areas of paint programmed to be 'missing,' and, though I cannot hear it over the din, I bet there's a beautifully-composed and artificially-responsive engine noise. Trying to blend in. Oh no we can't let the *poors* see us can we. No, we just go in, and beat up boys, and leave, squeezing our way through this disgusting *rabble* till we reach the big clear roads where the poors cannot afford the tolls, and then home, to our ethereal mansion on the hill, propped above the layer of smog and fug like a stylite's pole in the desert, above all that, do you see, we're *above* all that...

"Oh, I hate him so much," I sigh. "I hate all of them."

"I know."

"God. So *satisfying* to say what I fucking mean sometimes."

"You should try being dead. You can say anything you want any time you want. And you don't get written up."

"Mm. Pros and cons, though, darling."

"Swings and roundabouts."

The car is moving slowly for now, but I swing up the binoculars again and widen the field of view. "The road opens up in about two...hm. Three miles."

"No, there's construction there."

"There isn't anything. Look."

She doesn't, and frowns. "Come on. Bring those."

We climb down a different ladder on the other side of the roof, scraping my palms in the rush, and jump down five or six feet into a shallow drift of muddy sand. I remember these too: meticulously scraped up by the streetcleaners and set aside for the local brickies and builders, trying to shore up the more obviously collapsing buildings where possible. Nothing goes to waste in the city.

A group of kids scatters as we approach, not afraid of us exactly but startled, I think, by unexpected novelty: two strange women, one in questionable shape, in long gowns of silver and red.

"Hey!" Win calls, the twang of her neighbourhood accent

returning. "Who wants to earn a coupla stiks?"

Two boys and a girl return in curious little hops, like sparrows, the others showing nothing more than the soles of their runners. Win taps the inside of her wrist. "Two now. Three when you get back."

The taller boy shakes his head. The other, his grey t-shirt smeared with fish guts, opens his mouth and closes it again. The girl, smaller than the other two, shrugs, and taps the inside of her wrist the way you do, the return gesture, just above her wristband. The flesh where the wiring is embedded looks puffy and white, as if her hands have been soaking in the canal. How it goes. She says, "What you need, ep?"

Win gives her the stiks: a local brand, I notice with a faint, faraway pang of yearning, and flavoured. Ginger! No, we're not allowed. Let me minimize my sins, it's bad enough I'm out here in the first place.

The little girl pockets them and looks up expectantly. Win digs in her pockets for something else, a small dark disc scribbled with circuitry, and says, "Ep-ep, I need you to go put something on a car."

"A car?"

"One car. With a monster in it."

For the dead travel fast, she says, but we have taken too long on our mission of justice, heading to Draavik's, doing what she declared needed to be done, returning. It is twelve-fifteen, I am late, I am filthy, I am wild and roaring with exhilaration, I am much changed in ways I have not even realized, I do not wish to think of them, my hair is disarrayed from the getaway flight in our stolen hover (a fizzing heap of rubble now being disassembled by an industrious hive of pickers and their kids, the rest in a canal over in Upper Yarlen), it will take an hour to make me presentable, two to make me worth my fee, and of course I have been noticed, and Serpentine and Jasper do not even bother calling me into their office to reprimand me; they simply have one of the maids bring me a letter on a brass tray engraved with skulls and flowers.

Yesterday, I think, such an envelope would have killed me. Before even opening it I would have sobbed, pleaded innocence, found excuses, sickened myself with guilt and worry, and started planning an elaborate compensation to the client I had failed...today, I tear it open and suffer the slow revolution of my stomach, once, twice, because you do not abandon the habits of obedience and self-umbrage so easily, the owners of the House of Bicchieri are *disappointed*, they are *hurt*, they are trying to understand that perhaps I did not feel well after my friend was taken for medical care (there's that passive voice again), but the client comes first, always, the client always comes first (yes, and usually only, thank you), so they have no choice but to take a fine from the account that pays my wages, room, and board, because it's not about you, do you see, and it's not about him, it is about our *reputation*, which we need in order to keep operating, but since it is only your first major offense, we are being lenient, because we *do* care about you, we care about *all* our employees.

Bastards.

The actual number is on the back of the letter, and for a moment through my shocked and ringing ears I feel a neutral curiosity about this. I have been here for eleven years and never heard the precise amounts, we do not usually talk money, it is seen as crass, something only poor people do, won't Winfield laugh when I tell her what they have docked me...

But the number winds me like a punch and I have to look at it again when my vision returns, see where the decimal point falls.

For several minutes there is no sound anywhere but the noise of my heart, gulping and palpitating as it falls into my guts. Stop it, I say faintly. Be reasonable. Stop overreacting.

What have you done, I say, as if I have left my body, as if I am addressing this slumped sallow dirty thing clutching the pristine paper from several feet away. What have you done, you fucking fool. All this for a...for a violent lark, a prank almost.

Oh my God. Oh my God. Oh my God.

Stop it! It's just a number. It's just...it doesn't mean anything. It's just money.

No it isn't. It isn't just money. It's the food I eat the bed I sleep on the roof over my head my medication my showers my

Stop! Panicking won't do you any good.

I'll go to them, I'll tell them the truth, I'll—

Stop it.

Oh God oh God. And for a second I even think, and there's a little high giggle that certainly did not come out of my mouth, that I should kill myself, that maybe I'll come back too, like Winfield, maybe her god will speak to me...there's nothing more dangerous (the city teaches us) than someone who's got nothing left to lose.

But someone who's got nothing left to lose who is given a generous, open-ended offer to earn it all back with hard work is not dangerous at all. Is desperate, groveling, speechlessly obedient. Splayed heart and soul for inspection and approval (and money, always money).

You can take extra shifts, the letter says. Flexibility is very important to us (ha!). Immediately I start doing the calculations. I could cut out lunch and dinner, just eat breakfast (the meal that puts me the least in the hole anyway), so that's two hours back, not quite two hours... an hour and forty minutes. No more naps. How long can you survive on two or three hours of sleep a night? Amalthea does it. Elizabeth does it. Or they say they do, I don't know. I could train myself to do it.

More than a decade and I haven't learned anything here, have I. No I haven't.

And it's all been taken away. But I could get it back.

If I just behave. If I forget everything I did today, everything that's happened, put my head down, get back in the traces, back to work. Forswear and disavow it.

Is this worth it? Worth the stunned glee in Nero's eyes when I tell him what we did, show him the video, or worth his stunned silence when I tell him what it cost me?

No, of course not, says the prim little Jewel inside my head: the pocket expert in her white lab coat, who often says sensible, data-backed things and is very good at math. Of course it's not worth it. You fucking idiot. You impulsive fucking idiot. As if you were in love and had lost all your damn sense. Aren't you ashamed of yourself?

Yes, I tell her. I am. Very. It turns out. Yes. Ashamed beyond belief.

Was it worth it? What does worth mean? says the little Winfield inside my head, a fairly new resident.

You're one to talk, I tell her. You still decked in your silk and your gold.

I take a couple of deep, heaving breaths, and gather my things, and go to see who can lend me a few credits so I can buy a hot shower. I stink of blood and canals and no one will want me. There's still much to lose, there's so much to lose. You have to choose what constitutes an acceptable loss. I can do that. I'm the fucking adult around here.

Ten

Weeks pass while I keep my head down. Win, meanwhile, does the opposite of whatever I am doing. The city is in uproar and she is photographed wearing a full-face mask of black that I recognize, at once, as a piece of engineered cashmere sliced from Draavik's suitjacket as we left his mansion.

She had laughed doing it, the real trophy was the video I had taken on her phone, the one we surreptitiously showed Nero in his hospital bed, but she had wanted something she could touch. Disgusting, I thought then. Worse now, I think. That bloodsoaked scrap of cloth pressed to her face the way Pederssen's hands had been, how could she stand it?

But her posture tells the true story: more than erect, actually arrogant, no more charm school 'top of the head to the heavens!' but pelvis out, a snarl behind the oval of soft black wool. Beautiful Narcissus saw his own reflection in the pool and drowned, unable to resist his loveliness. You're so beautiful, he said, and took a breath to say something else, but what he breathed in was his death.

That would never happen to Winfield. She conceals the beauty of her face. In that small and apparently utterly still mythological pool she would see only this darkness, two eyes burning behind it like coals.

The act of covering her face said something else, too; it said *See who I am*. Because we all knew it was her, and that meant the owners did too. It could not be anyone else but her. Even if she was dead.

"Those two won't do anything," Nero says when I show him the paper, folded to the photograph and stained somewhat with jam. "How can they? It's impossible. No one will believe them. They'll be put away."

"Where?"

"I don't know. Wherever they put people like them."

"The canals would be too good for them."

"Yes. Poor fish. Think of the fish, eating them. But I suppose they're used to garbage on the menu." He perspires with pain as the broken bone heals, as the nerves find new places in the crushed synthetic material to grow into; he looks unsteady, nauseated. I or a few of the others visit him daily, cajoling him to eat. I cannot really spare the time, I am working flat-out, exhausted, but somebody's got to do it. He won't eat if we don't watch.

I am angry at the thought that somewhere, Draavik's broken arms and legs must be nearly knitted back together, as good as new, maybe better than new, while he is being lavished with drugs; they have machines that do all that, robots. To the rest of the city the medicine of the rich looks like magic. I hate it. I hate him. I hated the sounds the bones made as they broke, I stumbled over the bodies of his guards and retched into one of his potted plants when Win did it. I hated his screams because they meant he lived.

Pederssen lives too and I hate him too. I am filled with so much hate sometimes that I wonder that whatever rich bastard grunts and pants above me cannot smell it coming through my skin. But maybe that's how you get rich or at least how you stay rich: you ignore that smell, which is given off by everyone around you. If you're rich you can always buy something nicer to smell.

"Her name is Georgia," Nero murmurs, and forks up a piece of ham. "Your nemesis."

"She's not my nemesis. She is, at best, a minor pain in my

ass."

"Well, she's a terrible spy," he says. "She's got a big mouth. Can't shut up. Iris is looking after most of Win's jewelry now? And she says your little stool pigeon spends all her time searching Win's room for it. And asking about her. 'Oh, who was here before me? She had wonderful taste. She must have been lovely!' Bullshit. Win had the taste of a brain-damaged magpie."

I roll my eyes. The spy, unsubtle as she is, must be getting frantic now without anything new to bring to the owners. I've been a perfect straight arrow, a dead-end with a blank wall. No secret doors here, I would tell her if I confronted her.

But I am all done with confrontation and conflict. I am all done with vengeance and payback. Everything is paid back, the accounts of morality are squared away now, and I need to put my life back together after what I did. "Win won't come back here," I say. "No matter what. It's over."

"I know. She's smarter than that."

"I'll come back tonight," I say, and kiss his forehead, leaving an expensive rainbowy print. "You have to eat."

"I eat."

"Pretend you're a monster fish," I say. "Or pretend that you're an ordinary fish. Eating monsters."

"Don't patronize me, whore."

"Go on and starve then." I flounce out to his hooting laughter. These micro-performances keep us going, they always have, we all of us love the tiny one-act plays enacted over the last spoonful of jam at breakfast, a new pair of shoes, the glossy surficial frivolity of our ordinary lives. This place, the House of Bicchieri, was a restaurant once, centuries ago. Then, and I think this is important, it was a theatre.

Winfield is not play-acting though; she is doing something else, something deeper, older. A tragedy, in five acts. And she knows it, too. Out there in her shredded gown and her stolen mask.

I think of our mad rush back to the House in Draavik's stolen hover, skimming the canals, shrieking as the gelatinous water splattered up at us in slow-moving lumps, dislodging startled fish, nine-legged frogs, floating garbage, semi-sapient mats of algae. The little wooden boats dodging and rocking in our rippled wake, their curses and cheers following us because it seemed that we were persecuted and that is who and what you cheer for in the city. Freedom. The freedom to be covered with filth, and to move fast.

I think: Hamlet? Othello? Macbeth? Who are you, my strange new friend? What died, and was replaced by the words of a god?

I think: No. It doesn't matter any more.

Eleven

One client with a two-hour appointment cancels and I find myself temporarily adrift, paid my percentage of the cancellation fee, so not technically not making money, but boneless and limp at the audacity of free time, of having money but not doing the work, not even the work of sitting in one of the stupid gazebos listening to some ass in a suit talk about his stock portfolio and smelling the lavender (and if you don't think it's work listening to a man talk, come take one of my shifts sometime).

I head out to the pool, clamber into an alligator floaty, stare up through the discreet gleam of the dome above us. Insects don't like it but birds don't seem to mind, and today there are several sparrows and one radiant starling, its natural iridescence multiplied and refracted through the coating on the plastic as if it has been dipped in oil. Where is your flock? Whoever saw a starling by itself? This is an omen, I tell myself. I'll have to ask Nero what it means.

But it is an omen, because a few minutes later Serpentine and one of her assistants, which she goes through at a rate of about four per year, enter the dome.

Serpentine claps her hands, so heavy with rings that it sounds like a drum riff. All around me damp and sleepy heads rise from lawn or water, indolent, fuzzy with pool chemicals, so that I think of bees coming out of the flowers on the lawn. "Everyone? Everyone! Special announcement!"

Here it comes. It what? I don't know. She's looking right at me, though she's not facing me: I study the sleek sunken paperwhite face, the richly leonine mass of her hair over the long embroidered caftan.

Right at me. You can tell even through the sunglasses, her gaze like two hot points of light on my skin, and I will myself to transmute into something heavy—lead, mercury, particarb, stone—and sink to the bottom of the pool. Inhale. Narcissus dead drowned turned into a flower, oops.

But I float and smile, in my white swimsuit printed with oranges and lemons. Here it comes.

"We're holding a fête!" she says, smiling broadly. What beautiful teeth she has.

It takes me a second to parse what she said, as I stared. Well, all right. A party? All right. We like parties. I do wish I had money for a new gown, new shoes, new gloves maybe (gloves are very in this season). I'm nowhere near paying back my fine though, and only just (maybe in the last day or so) at the point where I don't need to borrow money from people to eat. All this, for one strike. My first strike in eleven years. You see how they do it.

"What's the occasion, Miss Serpentine?" Georgia calls. "Have we been very good?" Several of us pucker our lips sweetly at each other: *Asskisser.* Iris chuckles and submerges to hide her laughter. The water surges around me as she swims in circles, which is another way of laughing, like a shark.

"It's Miss Aventurine now," Serpentine-now-Aventurine snaps. I sigh, and wonder if Jasper has changed his name too. She says, "It's a new occasion. Something that I think we'll make a bit of a tradition. Traditions are important, you know. Only humans have those. Not animals. So it's meaningful, developing a new one. We're calling it a Celebration of Life. And guess where it'll be held?"

Passive voice again. But even before she speaks, I know. And something hits me square in the gut, something with weight and mass that I did not think was real in the sense that it possessed those things, or real in the sense that it really existed: blasphemy. The profaning of something sacred. No, there is nothing sacred to us...*yes, there is*. There is the one thing. Of which we never speak, because it is ours, belongs to us, and someone has told her the secret, the location, maybe even (Christ!) our rituals and our...but that's why she said it. A tradition.

The spy? No, even she would not have. Would she? It is unfathomable. I feel again that thing I tried to push down: this hunger for revenge that has no single name in our language. The way it lights up every nerve ending like being struck by lightning, so that all I can think of is telling everyone else to look away, and striding over to Georgia, and holding her head underwater till she is dead.

Stop it.

Stay calm.

It is too much to hope that Aventurine will burst into flames upon stepping across the threshold, or that the long-abandoned structure will fall in on her (and Jasper too, don't forget him, they move as one, they hunt as one). Such things are for old stories. But if you were the devil, and you set foot on sacred ground...and of *course* it's not sacred, her entire body says, her smug tone as she talks. Of course it's not sacred. Nothing that belongs to *you* has any whiff of the divine. You cannot create such a thing and so it is ours to take and sully.

I have been to twenty funerals there, nineteen deaths. My friends, my enemies, my competitors, my students. People who had wept with me and eaten with me and bled with me and tried to build our little shelter against the great cold unfeeling night of money that presses down on us in this House. We have nothing to love but each other.

You cannot feel love, says the speech under Aventurine's speech. You? Not you. Not any more than an animal can.

For a second I am wild with anger and I wonder how I ever thought of self-destruction when it is so clear that it is the world that needs to be thrown off something high, and that is when I know: they are throwing a party there not just to break us and hurt us and insult us without recrimination, because that is what bullies like to do, but to lure Winfield there and trap her. The House is a cage, after all. They know about cages.

Winfield will know. That it is a trap, I mean. But sometimes what you want in the trap is worth the crunch of the iron jaws around your leg...I lie very still and dabble one hand in the water, my mind racing. Sometimes you want the bait more than you want to live.

Of course they will invite Pederssen and of course he will come. Even if he knows Win wants her revenge, he will still come. To gloat and to be invincible and untouchable: to be the new god of our church. You're allowed to hate gods, after all. Because they are allowed to smite you.

They will catch her no matter how wily she is and they will kill her again or put her away or simply take her apart, for science or for sadism, and life will go back to normal.

"Jewel!"

I shade my eyes with my hand. Aventurine is standing near the edge of the pool where I have drifted in my silent, pondering panic. My face must scream murder. I rearrange it into something obedient and pleasant. "Yes, Miss Aventurine?"

"I'm putting you in charge of the entertainments. Do let me know if you need any guidance."

"Of course. Thank you for the honour." I've done that before, there should be nothing strange in the request, nothing sinister. There are only five or six companies to call around. They send their demo troupes (singers, acrobats, contortionists, anatomists) and you pick a few acts.

But she keeps staring at me, her smile unceasing. Don't, I think. You'll ruin that expensive thread-job that smoothed out your nasolabial folds last year. That's a lot of money. It's hard to erase the marks of human emotion. That's our money, you know. Earned on our backs. Stop staring, you gargoyle. Stop it. You know I was a friend of Win's, you think I'm in cahoots with her somehow. The escaped courtesan who crisscrosses the city on rooftops and canals, who walks underwater unafraid of drowning, who steals and lies, who rescues people, ends fights, stabs rapists, who the people love, who you hate. The shameful secret you share with her and him binding you all together. One big happy.

You know it's her. You know it's me. But you don't know what she can do now. Do you?

It doesn't matter, her smile says. Whatever she is, she will be a prisoner. And thanks to her you will be punished in whatever ways don't affect our profits. Making you clap for a dancing dog act in your sacred place would be a start. Or maybe making you beg...

"Do a good job," she says, "and maybe we can have a little chat about your... performance improvement plan. Hmm?"

Play along, she means. Dance for us and we'll throw you a coin. Aiming for your face. "That would be lovely, Miss Aventurine."

We remain silent as she leaves, the assistant tossing one last, desperate look back at us. The sun through the dome makes their shadows multifarious: like they are centipedes walking upright.

Now they will be watching me, I think, and Nero too, and a few of the others. To see how we will give Winfield this news.

But they will watch in vain. She'll find out, but we will not need to give her this information. It will escape from the House like radon and something inside Win will be set off and beep. I know it.

Somewhere across the city, she has looked up and said: *He will be there and I will kill him.*

Twelve

"Not just him," Nero says when I come to his room the day before the party. His wing has been deemed healed, and it certainly opens and closes, and looks nice, but he winces horribly as he flexes it. "Them too. S... Aventurine and whatever the hell he's calling himself this week. Agate or whatever."

"Them? No, I don't think so."

"Yes. When have you ever known her to take half-measures? Look at what she does to people in this city who fuck people up. Look at what she did to Draavik. An eye for an eye. And then some."

"Well, yes," I say uneasily. "But that wasn't because she got carried away, darling. I was there. It was because she knew you had saved for the wings for so long. Because you had gone without."

"Nearly a year," he muses. His room is dim, fragrant, spotless; only the faux-baroque ornamentation of the moulding, and a dozen bottles of creams and unguents on his vanity, catch the light. His wallpaper is like mine, purple verging on black, with twisting, tumbling designs worked in some kind of flocked stuff. He doesn't have a window, even the tiny token one that some of us have, just an enormous blistered mirror that takes up an entire wall, its gilt frame carved with leering faces.

We sit together on his chaise, fists between our knees, hunched over as if we are in great pain. He says, "This is something else, isn't it? It's one thing to just rough people up. Hell, I've got a whole list of clients who like that kind of treatment. She could make a mint if she came back. *Get your licks from a dead gyal!* But murdering him. I don't know. I thought she'd have given up by now. When she realized he's too hard to get to."

I nod hopelessly. That is what the fête has done to me, I think: taken the last of my hope. For what? For everything. I thought I had a future once. But she will take it away if she comes. "What are we going to do?"

"What?"

"About all this. About her. Tomorrow."

He doesn't move, but I feel his dense familiar body withdraw from me anyway, retracting like the poked eye of a snail from a salty fingertip. The body produces these salts; there's nothing you can do about it even if you do not mean offense. That's the impression I get, in those few hurt seconds: that his very soul is pained, and must flee me. "If you're going to say something you'll be ashamed of later," he says evenly, "then don't say it."

"I won't then."

"Good."

He thinks I'm a coward, a traitor. He thinks I will sabotage Win's mission somehow, that I will collude with the owners to bring her down and stuff her in a cage, that I will shove Georgia aside to grovel at their feet hoping for redemption.

Do you think so little of me, I want to say, then check whether I would be ashamed of it and so fail his test: Yes. I am ashamed.

Like you're so much better than me, I want to blurt, like *you're* the one setting some kind of moral standard. You set her loose on Draavik. You did that.

Can't say that either.

So, by his metric, there's nothing left to say. I get up and go back to my own room.

Thirteen

Here is where we are expected (not even requested: *required*) to show off our wit and talent and potential. Here is where we must say to clients: We're not like those other houses. Small-h. Brothels really. With their tacky little escorts. What *you* want is a courtesan. What *you* want is to get what you pay for. Our entire demeanour must say this at all times.

I am in a couple of different kinds of pain and I conceal everything under my most dazzling and calculated act: a veteran of the house, experienced in things you've never heard of (no, I assure you, you have not), capable of astonishing feats in a one-hour session, unbelievable perversities in two. Educated, erudite, able to converse on numerous topics, offer advice, stock picks, a listening ear, as well as the warmth and softness of my plump, welcoming golden body. Eleven years, yes.

But I am in pain and the pain is an insult cutting into me like a scalpel, redhot, even white-hot, but refusing to sear my nerve-endings shut. The bastards have drained the church and reinforced the iffy ceiling with carbon-fiber struts, cheap-looking and ugly against the ancient dignified wood, the name of the manufacturer clearly visible in ultra-reflective white against the gray hexagons, as if we've plastered the place with ads. They have unbolted the pews from the floor and shoved them to the periphery of the room, a jumbled mess. The altar where we place the coffin is a buffet table. All our votives and candles are gone, decades of painstaking placement and shuffling and arrangement. The small narratives we made on the walls are painted over in flat black.

The place has been profaned and every time I look around and see what they have done I feel the double-punch of *How dare they* followed by *How dare I be offended*. It's not a real church. It's not a real religion. It used to be something once and then we took it over because they said we could have nothing else, nothing. I am angry and then I am angry that I am angry. And all of this I have to shove under the cool surface of my smile, and hold its head there till it stops struggling.

Nero has acquired a fan club, people cooing over and even petting him: his curls, his wings, the thick silk of his suit which is cut so closely I am not even sure he can sit down in it; he stood in the bow of the yacht on the way here.

He looks, to a trained eye, half out of his mind with insult. Like me, I think. But also like me, he knows better than to drop the act. Our sanctuary has been violated, the soul driven from it, but we go on. Dancing with clients, complimenting their outfits, asking after the health of their portfolios. Feeding them little tid-bits from the buffet table, sweetly declining sips from their drinks (no one wants to hear all our alcolarms go off at the same time; the roof will collapse from the noise, reinforced or no).

Win hasn't come and it is nearly midnight, when our coaches will turn back into pumpkins, and probably the bulk of the guests will begin to trickle in. The party has been going on for hours already. Since sunset, and the slow dissipation, by agonizing increments, of the day's heat and humidity. My makeup feels like it's going to slide off my face in a single unit and plop onto the floor. Like the cream tart Samira dropped earlier, causing (forcing, really) us all to make the same joke at the same time.

I hold down a hysterical giggle and accept a waltz from a client too tall for me to even see his face in the dim light. He stinks of some metallic cologne, as if under his tux he is a robot sweating molten aluminum, and his hands are small and wet.

The music, from floating speakerlights, comes down ghostly and slow, like snow rather than sound. Particle, wave. Great gusts of incense like the hot scented breath of a dragon occasionally blow in from the loaded braziers outside, meant to cut the stink of the lapping water.

We're slumming it, the guests say, and giggle in scandalized delight. Oh, *isn't* it risqué. Some of them, Agate is saying, through peals of laughter, sneak down here and throw parties after funerals. Oh, like when we have wakes, someone else says. Can you *believe* it? Aventurine says. Isn't it perfectly adorable? Monkey see, monkey do. Gales of laughter. Imagine creeping down here. Leaving the House and. When there are three enormous, lovely rec rooms to. And they can. Or they could. But instead.

Nothing is holy to you, I think, and that is all right: make it be all right within yourself. Nothing is holy to me either.

Not after going to them, and telling them everything I knew about Winfield and where she hid and hunted and swindled and traded. Not after I prostrated myself trying to bargain for her strange small reinstituted life. (Hers, I said. So it would sound less craven than mine. So I would not have to say out loud *What must I do to regain your favour and keep my job.*)

Please, I said, in the darkness of their study, surrounded by their trinkets, the fan blowing their hideous scent at me. She's made mistakes. Please go easy on her.

Jewel, we are honourable people, Aventurine said proudly, and in the circle of her voice I had heard myself included: We all, *and* you, are honourable people. We'll keep our word. And you are so worried about your friend. Well of course you are. We were nearly out of our minds with grief too. You remember that.

Well, no, I thought. I still think: No. I don't think so.

I told them she would come by water. I told them she stole hovers and boats. But I did not tell them about this church and our secret post-death necessities. That was someone else. We are all ragged with rage and insult at the blasphemy, we all feel that our insides have been torn out and picked through, to have these rich fucks dancing in our holy place, mocking our broken-down sanctuary.

I didn't have much to trade anyway, I imagine myself telling
Nero defiantly, hotly, my face aflame with rectitude. I'm trying
to save her. It's barely more than the papers have been saying
anyway. I did nothing wrong.

There's no god that can hear us but I still think again and
again as I twirl in circles, God I wish tonight were over. God
please let it be over. Please in my next blink let me wake up
in my room, in my own bed, on fresh sheets. No atheists in
ratholes. Isn't that the saying?

Agate and Aventurine sometimes favour me with their smiles
and I swing wildly between genuinely relieved pleasure, and a
disgusted flinch, as if I have been threatened by a growling dog.
Showing your teeth means different things at different times, I
tell myself. Calm down. Nothing lasts forever. This party won't
last forever. This hateful charade.

You people can't love, they said when I spoke to them in their
study. Not *real* love. So it is not that you loved this place or your
silly games. It's something else. Was something else. And you'll
feel whatever that is again. For something else. Later.

All right. If that's true. If. Then get through tonight.

I am handed off, smoothly stolen into someone else's arms, a
gallant thief: Nero, tired and haggard under an artful coating
of glitter. "God, my feet fucking hurt," he says. "Is this over yet?
Have they made their point?"

"Mine too. And these are my best shoes. Iris even put foam in
the back. Fuck these rich fucks."

"Ugh. Not without an appointment."

We dance through the other couples, barely moving. My back
hurts too, and my neck. And my face, from smiling. I lean on
his silken lapel and close my eyes for a moment, the closest thing
I've felt to rest for about twenty hours. Annoyed, the collagen
armature of my bra implant senses the change in position and
hoiks everything up into their preprogrammed position, a twang
of pain in my back where it attaches. Stay perky! Stay up! Fuck
off. I hope no one heard the hydraulics.

With every minute that goes by we are safer and Winfield is
safer. Go be a hero somewhere else, I hear Nero think. Go beat
rich people up somewhere else, I think.

I don't know if I'd call it heroism. Maybe it is. I don't want
to think about it. What does it mean to kill a murderer? Why
does she get to be the one who does it? Maybe because she is the
only one who can? Maybe being a murder victim gives her the
right? This must be the first time it's ever happened. But I don't
know how to make any of it sit right in my head. We were more
accepting of her resurrection than her lust for vengeance, and
what kind of people does that make us?

He's killed others, I'm sure he has. I have only glimpsed
Pederssen a few times in person, sometimes in the paper, but if
you had asked me, beforehand, whether he would be the one
who caused one of our dawn funerals, I would have said yes. No
hesitation.

There are no courts, there are no lawyers. Those are things
we read about in books, so I know they were real at some point,
but not any more. There is law but it does not apply to everyone,
and that itself is enshrined in law. The law says: Only you and
you. Not you. People could not fight it when it happened not
merely because fighting it was outlawed but because they were
too hungry and too ill and there was simply no recourse; because
if you had to choose between a fight you could not win, and
trying to feed yourself and your family, you made the choice. An
easy one. I had done it, growing up. Most of us have.

Another yachtful of people must have arrived; I feel the
room increase in density, the cross-currents change. New
scents, another stifling cloud of incense billowing in as if it had
an invitation too. The way a crowd is a crowd even when it is
entirely silent and you're not looking at it, so that you cannot be
surprised by it when you turn a corner and see it. My childhood:
spent trying not to be surprised by things, and failing.

"Oh, Christ," Nero whispers into my ear. I don't need him to
tell me what he's seen; the skin between my shoulderblades itches
as if something is about to be driven into it. The feel of a healing
implant. Something small but sinister, something that could go
very wrong, kill you. I resist a powerful urge to reach up and
scratch, worried for the fingertips of my borrowed lace gloves.

My stomach feels cold and heavy, sinking with a certain liquid
grace, like cold water coming down from melting ice. Whatever

happens next will not surprise me, I think, and then it does happen and I am not surprised.

"Oh, Mr. Pederssen! How was your trip here?" Agate cries.

"Did you enjoy the quartet? They came very highly recommended," Aventurine adds.

They think boot polish gives you magical powers and the more you lick the closer you come to god. It's not money they want. Already they are rich, by any stretch of the imagination. They want other things from him, things you cannot measure, and they want them desperately. If it were the other kind of fête they'd be fellating him right now, here in the church. Or, more realistically, getting one of us to do it. Gratis.

Nero says, "There's the bait. Look at him."

"No, I don't want to look. Just tell me."

"Well, don't then. Smug enough to make you puke onto my nice new suit. Because they helped him cover it up, they're on the same team, they're *buddies*. They're not ashamed. Why should they be? It's not like we're real people."

"Nero."

"It's not like he killed a *person*, you know, Jewel. He just busted a business asset."

"*Nero.*"

"Like breaking a chair at a bar. Oh, God," he whispers in a new tone, fresh horror, "brace yourself, darling."

But I don't need to, I am already comprehensively braced, my back is ready for this, my tits are ready for this, their internal cantilever creaks and groans under the strain of how straight I am standing and how ready for the blow to come.

The owners appear as two gleaming skulls in the gloom, a brief glitter of teeth, and then I am moved bodily out of Nero's arms and placed in position to dance with Pederssen. The acrobats swoop and soar behind him, sparkling like dragonflies, like the big blue and gold ones that pick up dropped food on the canals before it can sink. I note this mechanically, wondering if I am about to drop dead, my heart is beating so fast.

Pederssen is much bigger than I remember him being and this seems relevant not merely in the sense that I feel intensely and personally and viscerally threatened, as if I have placed my hand into the jaws of a street dog, but in the sense that it forces a movie to play in my mind that I have not seen and am therefore forced to imagine: the way he held Win down with one hand and covered her face with the other until she was dead, the way it would have cost him no effort, the way merely the size of his hands and the weight of his body would have done it, the way he would have ignored her kicking and pleading and scratching and writhing until it all stopped.

His face is monstrously pleased, the expression so twisted under his blonde-and-silver hair that it looks as if it's been transplanted from another species. Some kind of bird or lizard. Blandly lipless, the effect of a smile given by the malevolent shape of the jaw. Don't talk to me, I think. I'm not responsible for what happens next if you do.

He says, "I've heard so much about you, Jewel."

"Oh, how flattering," I say automatically. Absolutely automatic: like jerking the hand back from a flame.

"I'll have to remember to book an appointment later on to find out if it's all true."

"Oh, it is true. All of it."

"You know, your owners speak very highly of you," he growls, leaning close. His breath is loaded with whiskey. Heavy enough on the smoke to be the exhalation of a dragon. He doesn't seem drunk, look drunk. My hand creaks in his. "Of your... experience. Compared to some of the other bitches. Do you find that's helpful? Hm? Experience versus youth?"

"Well, I think many people have natural talents at a young age," I say, and try to correct the high, panicked note in my voice, Winfield, he's talking about Win, they would have told him that she and I were friends, or something, what did they tell him, he knows, what does he know, does he know what he's here for? Does he know that? "But of course, training is helpful for all skills."

"They can't train you to want it. Can they. You just do on your own. That's why you do this. I know. They told me." His hand on my back moves down, squeezes a handful of flesh through my dress. I keep dancing, my face inches from his leer. "Hmm? Dripping for it. Aren't you. Not like her."

"Oh, Mr. Pederssen. You do know how to work up a girl."

His grip on my hand tightens, with both hands he is leaving bruises, his jeweled rings snagging both skin and fabric. He will draw blood soon from somewhere. A space clears around us, and I wonder about it till I realize that the others are subtly and gently and I hope unnoticeably steering their partners away from us, from the circle of contamination. The stink of murder. Nero, his curls visible above the crowd, looks at me despairingly before he is whisked away.

Under Pederssen's tuxedo jacket several weapons gleam in the low light, the glitter of metal or nanoceramic or LEDs, I am not sure, tucked into the flat silk pockets where other people might carry pills or creds. He doesn't need any of that. People of his level, people in the stratosphere of money, they carry their wealth with them in a way they never have to touch. How many bodyguards did he bring? To a party of indolent courtesans and other tuxed fucks? Two, maybe. Three. As a matter of habit, not because he fears the revenge of a dead girl. Why would he? Why would anyone? No, he is enjoying being bait that will never be touched.

My God, maybe she is not even real, maybe her resurrection is something we made up. Maybe she died and was properly interred and I have been hallucinating from grief this whole time...but if so then maybe I can say something to him. Not something cutting, hurtful. He cannot be hurt by people like me. But something. In the gloom his eyes hold a stunning amount of light: blue but an engineered blue, like a satin dress, like a sapphire. The last thing Win would have seen.

I open my mouth and we crash through the ceiling.

Not in the abstract. Not metaphorically. It's so fast that my brain races to capture and register what is happening: things in the body move at the speed of chemicals, not light.

Panic. Weightlessness. Pain. Noise. Impact. *Impact*: then the sudden absence of all these and a thin high scream, mine, and gravity reasserts itself. I crash hard, something jabbing into my leg with a pop as the skin parts, and then I am rolling uncontrollably sky-sea-roof-sky-sea-roof and falling before I can process what I glanced at for just a second and what it might mean and then I have hit the thick icy water like a slab of concrete.

Breath knocked loose and escaping in thick bubbles, I kick instinctively but is it up? Where is up? Where has up gone?

I don't have much air left. Seconds. Water opaque as paint. A void.

A second later I figure out which way is *down*, in the utter darkness: because my gown is soaked and it is pulling me at speed like something has grabbed my ankle and is swimming as hard as it can for the ocean floor.

I can't hold my breath any more.

I will not come back. Not like Winfield. Up there on the roof of the church, garrotting Pederssen with the line she had tethered to the ancient steeple, his fingers already whitening, her shock realizing that I had reflexively clung to him when she snatched him, that we had flown up there together for no reason other than that I am always afraid to be alone, always, three angels ascending to heaven, ha ha, and now I am sinking, dying, I open my mouth and inhale and the kicking stops like a switch has been flicked and it *burns*, how can water *burn*, I deserve this, I deserve this.

if a god lives here help me please help me

if there is one maybe she will understand that

i have always thought that the punishment for any offense should be death

because i grew up seeing people die all around me in front of me i grew up thinking

a mistake meant death and because it was everywhere it must be all right

the grownups wouldn't let it happen if it wasn't all right to happen

if there is a god help me at least tell me which way is up if there is

a god do you know my friend do you know what you did to her do you

it hurts it burns

Fourteen

Light returns and I realize I am no longer in motion, perhaps have not been for some time. There is a stillness to everything, not just the negation of momentum but new inertia. My dress is soaked, ears full of a high steady tone. Light above me: not the moon but strings of coloured bulbs. Hovering? No. Tacked to the crumbling wood of some huge dark edifice.

Yes. A party. I have not gone far then, we are still at the church, I might still be alive.

I heave a dozen rattling breaths and spit and cough, and the thick rank water oozes from my mouth and nose. "Still going?" someone says near me, Nero squatting on the boardwalk next to me, flanked by two others, only half-paying attention, glancing back at the doors of the church, where people are congregating slowly, curiously, holding up gadgets or adjusting their glasses to film something within, as if they were watching a house on fire.

I croak out the obvious question.

"Not me," he says. "I didn't see who. Just look for whoever's wettest, I guess. But we'd better stay out h—Jewel, stop. Stop. Don't go in there!"

I shove him aside, clockworking back inside the church on stiff, numb legs, leaving a trail of blood behind me where the torn-up roof tore me up in turn, my chest on fire, lungs on

fire, throat on fire. Am I dead? I don't know. But I'm moving.
Someone catches at my trailing wrist, the strap of my gown,
seeking to slow me. I slap them away without looking. From
festive light into darkness, the music stopped, no one inside, the
few in the doorway with me staring, solemn, unmoving.

Did I hear screaming or did I only imagine it? Regardless, it
has stopped. Cables dangle from the ceiling like viscera,some
containing the bound and struggling forms of the bodyguards,
She will come by sea, I said, and she must have known I would say
that, I am transparent, useless. If she asks later I will say: No,
I lied to the owners with care and precision. I knew you better
than that. I knew you wouldn't bother fighting his people, but
would simply take him out of the place. Nobody else would have
known that. Only me. I fooled them good, didn't I?

Coward, traitor.

Pederssen is motionless on a thick quilt of blood. Did she cut
his throat? I can't tell in the gloom. There is a lot of blood, but
he is a very big man. And it's still spreading.

No one weeps; no one speaks. Winfield, glowing as if she
has doused herself in her perfume, stoops and flips open his
jacket, finding things, discarding them. Each rattle sounds like
a gunshot as the weapon hits the wooden floor. We few gawking
witnesses flinch, wince, as if we have been shot. It is too loud for
this solemnity.

Murdered him in our sacred place, how fucking dare you too.
How dare you. Why did you not do it in his house. Why here, in
the trap.

But she has circumvented the trap somehow; no bodyguards
lunge for her, no rentacops get out their tasers and deafeners.
And what are you going to do against the dead anyway. It is as
if we have all agreed to this: all agreed to disarm ourselves and
allow this to happen. Not justice but revenge.

One murder in here appears to be enough. She glances at
Aventurine, Agate, holding something small and dark in her
bloodied hands. "Outside," she says. "Now."

Pederssen croaks and gurgles and we draw back, startled, is
he resurrecting too, will he try to kill her in retaliation for killing
him in retaliation for killing her, who will win the prize in this

tontine—he reaches into his hip pocket and we scatter in silence, flocking like starlings away from the door, the shot is dull rather than sharp, a *phut*, another, *phut phut phut* until it's gone ten times and she is hit more than once, the other projectiles, whatever they are, thudding into wet wood, pinging off carbon fiber, but she doesn't look back, continues to shepherd the owners outside, down the aisle of the church towards me, a reverse wedding, not the joining of two lives but the ending of them. I can see all of her ribs as she approaches.

My heart is stuttering, all rhythm lost. It's too much. I cough, tasting salt, motor oil, iodine, other things. If what you have done is unforgivable you may as well just keep doing unforgivable things, her posture says, hips swinging, pelvis front. If no one's going to forgive you *anyway*. You may as *well*.

This is something the old Winfield would have said, I think with a sudden twitch of pain, the pain of memory. Maybe she did say it and that's why I'm thinking it. She did something unforgivable with a client. Maybe gross, or humiliating. But then you *may as well* do it again.

"I'm sorry." She halts a few paces from where I pant and cough and drip and hold out one hand as if it'll make a difference. "I didn't know you were there. That he still had you."

"Forgiven. But Win..."

But what? Agate and Aventurine are not merely accomplices in many murders. They're practically murderers themselves. If you cover it up the murderers keep going and going and going... how many lives have they thrown away as having less worth than the lives that took them? Telling people, *It's all right if it happens at the House of Bicchieri. We'll make it all right.* How many of my friends would still be alive?

I am shivering, I probably am in shock, I don't know who pulled me out, I didn't hear the voice of a god, I wish I had seen her face, I wish she could have appeared and told me it was going to be all right. "Please don't."

"Don't what?"

"Don't...kill them too."

She stares at me, honestly baffled. A moment passes. There's not much to think about, I suppose. Not more than about a moment's worth. "Get out of the way, Jewel."

"If you do this, you're no better than them."

"Thought you might say that." She brushes past me, shoving them through the door and onto the rickety boardwalk where my wet outline still shines in the party lights like a heap of wet laundry was deposited there. "What a boring saying. When has that ever convinced anyone? In a movie, maybe. I don't *care* if I'm better than them. It's not a contest."

"Winfield!"

Nero finally manages to grab me as I follow them, the three figures receding to where the last yacht bobs prettily in the unclean water. She glances back at me only when they are cornered between the end of the boardwalk and her, holding the gun or whatever it is she took from Pederssen's jacket. It looks a bit like a gun, a tiny one.

A quick, neat death. Much nicer than hers. She is so kind, the gun seems to say. Isn't she kind?

My heart will not slow, my whole body stings as if it's full of salt, and now at last my leg has started to hurt, though I know it has been bleeding for a while. People gather around me, enemies and friends. In the dark, clouded night, everyone seems to hold their breath. Maybe they think it is part of a show, our guests. Maybe they think this is modern art. One of the entertainments I arranged.

Nero is holding my wrist, his hand icy and slick. "Stop her!" he whispers.

"You stop her!"

She's still watching us and I don't know what to say. She'll laugh at whatever it is. Whatever moral high ground I try to find. And she'll say: You only said that to try to save your fucking job. That's what you want.

And I'll have to deny that it's the case, which it isn't, mostly, but it would not be fair to say it's entirely, it's just another thing I'll have to panic about after tonight but it is by no means first in the queue. The white boat gleams like a pearl, all its lights off except the ones marking out its body to others, bright red and green.

Wait. Maybe. Wait.

She's raising the gun. They face the water, unmoving. They haven't pleaded for their lives and I think that's probably good. It wouldn't stop her. But if I. Wait. Yes and the glow of their wristband displays. For they have them too. We all do. It proves that we're people worth keeping alive. That's how it works.

"Win!"

She doesn't turn. "What?"

Too many people are looking at me. It's a show, I want to scream. It's just another kind of show. I think I was *dead* a minute ago, all right? Fuck off. Go home. All of you. All of you.

"Don't kill them. Just...take them. Across the straits. To St. Maddwell. Take the boat, and take them across. Take their bands and dump them there."

"Why should I..." But the gun falls to her side, her finger loose on the trigger. Now Aventurine does protest, an incoherent wail. She's always been a little quicker on the uptake than her husband.

Strip their rings and necklaces and earrings away, their cards, their identity, their connections, whatever prestige or power they have accumulated by throwing us to the wolves for fourteen hours a day. Their House that lets them kill us and hush it up and starve unless we fuck our way into handouts. Strip that away. Let *them* starve. Start over from the bottom. And see how it goes.

To live well, they say, is the best revenge. But if it's suffering she wants in her revenge, why not let them suffer in the way that only life can manage?

Win chuckles, turning it over in her head, admiring the logic. She can make it, I think, so that they will never be able to access what they've got here. Lock them out. And why not?

She says, "*Well.* I've always wanted a yacht."

Fifteen

I don't know if it's a victory. There's nothing in the papers (and I am eternally curious as to who hushed it up; there is nothing scandalous about attending a party held by a House, nor is there about a public murder, but I suppose I must concede that there is about getting murdered, specifically, by someone you've murdered).

No one owns up to pulling me from the water. Weeks later, when I finally pluck up the nerve to ask, Nero says only that he saw me already on the boardwalk in the commotion as about half the party fled at Win's entrance, diverting smoothly around me like water around a stone. "Maybe it was a god," I tell him. "Winfield's god."

"Maybe. Are you a saint now?"

"You wouldn't respect me if I was a saint," I tell him. "And anyway, get thee behind me." He's got his eye on a new implant, horns. The ones that light up. Modelled on something exotic and long-extinct whose name I forget—ridged, delicate, spiraling horns in the catalogue. "You'll be Satan."

"I will not."

"Yes you will. An actual Satan. Like in a medieval manuscript."

"Well then we can charge extra."

"People will not pay extra to sleep with Satan."

"Will so." He drums his fingers on the windowsill, humming. I hate that we have become the new Aventurine and Agate, but it was true, infuriatingly, pathetically, inevitably true that we did still need jobs, and the code for everyone's wristbands had to be kept valid.

I dug into the reserves as soon as Win unlocked them, and tried to fix what I could (the two were sitting on a dragon's hoard of credits, the fuckers, as we'd always suspected despite their weepy speeches about operating on the slimmest, the most monofilament-whisper of margins every quarter).

We cancelled every appointment, in essence firing our clients; we're surviving on savings now. It was terrifying but necessary, and the fear we felt assured us we were doing the right thing. And a few of them contacted us quietly afterwards, promising nothing more than financial advice. "We could live on dividends," Nero said, and I said, "Some life."

Many of our friends left too, and I gave them as much cash as I could, even the loathsome Georgia, and wept when their wristbands blinked out of our system. Iris told me it didn't mean anything certain: only that they were out of range, perhaps returned to family or friends, or had picked up another job, not that they were dead. "You're too soft for this job," she said, but would not take it when I offered it to her. "It has to be you." At least I've got a secretary, I told her, as Nero sneered at me over the intercom.

We're actually making some money, even after everything, by opening up the South and the East Walks as botanical gardens, charging a nominal entrance fee for the clean air, the stupid gazebos, the faux marble statues of fauns and nymphs, the fountains, the flowers. I suppose we'll see how it looks in the spring. But even now, with everything fading and sere, people flock to it, rub their faces on the turf, photograph the drying ferns.

Win hasn't sent word.

Maybe she did kill them. No one here is a saint. And no one wants to be here. Not even those few of us who took pride in being good at what necessity had forced us to do. But it's the world we live in. It's the only way to survive: protect what we have, hold one another close and hold one another up.

Nero turns back from the window. "Are you busy later?"

"I'm a pimp, sweethead, I'm always busy."

"You can't call yourself a pimp. You're a girl."

"Well, a madame, then. And I just run the place, I don't... look, get to the point, Satan."

"I was thinking."

"I bet."

He flaps his hand impatiently at me. "About the church."

Even now the mention of it brings a rush of blood to my face that does not resemble grief but something else. Humiliation, embarrassment. Like someone reading my diary out over a megaphone. The sensible one, the one who never rocks the boat, suddenly exposed and vulnerable. Nero nods, seeing whatever it is that confirms what he wants to do: the flush, the tears. "We should take care of it," he says.

"Do you think so? Why us?"

"I don't know. Who else?"

Sixteen

I make him wait until nearly dawn, and we sail out there unremarked, unescorted, half-expecting at any moment to see Winfield drop from the broken rafters like a silver-gowned ghost. "Like the Phantom of the Opera," Nero says when I tell him. "But no. I don't think so. She'll be happy in St. Maddwell. It's a whole different setup over there."

"Is it?"

"Different enough, I think." He narrows his eyes. "Someone's waving. Do you know them?"

"Where?" I follow the line of his arm to a distant little flat-bottomed boat, sitting high on the sluggish, oily water. Again a pale flash of palm, a glimpse of a face in their lantern. The mudlark I saw in the city, the silhouette I keep telling myself I remember. I open my mouth to deny it, but if you see someone twice, if you nod at someone, isn't that enough of a connection these days? "Yes, a bit." I wave back at her.

Wet as the church is, steeped from foundation to windows with seawater, it still burns: hotly at the top, subdued and smoky at the bottom, twisting with curious colours from the centuries of salt, lichen, moss, chemicals, pollution, everything we deposited in it, everything the world deposited on it.

We tether the boat upwind and watch, the lanterns warm

and pink on our cold hands, it is not faith that is burning, it is
something else, and I don't feel sad as it begins to collapse and
vanish, it feels natural and good, like an animal sliding into the
sea from the beach, ready to swim away into the medium it has
always preferred.

What will we do for funerals now? Where will we make our
secret ceremony, we outcasts from everyone else's traditions?
I suppose I can ask about it when we get back, if there is
somewhere we might begin to pray to a newer god, one who
brings girls back from the dead to grant their greatest wish.

We hold our hands over the tiny candles and make smalltalk
about the unseasonable weather as the flames begin to die down.
It is supposed to snow next week. I believe it. It smells like snow.

acknowledgements

I would like to thank my agent, Michael Curry, and my editor dave ring, who truly understood the spirit and the voice of this piece. I would also like to thank our wonderful cover artist Carly Allen-Fletcher for doing the same. Finally, I am grateful to C.C. Finlay, whose thoughtful, incisive feedback helped me spot what I hadn't before, and hammer this into a stronger story!

About the Author

Premee Mohamed is an Indo-Caribbean scientist and speculative fiction author based in Edmonton, Alberta. She is the author of novels *Beneath the Rising* (2020) and *A Broken Darkness* (2021), and novellas *These Lifeless Things* (2021), *And What Can We Offer You Tonight* (2021), and *The Annual Migration of Clouds* (2021). Her short fiction has appeared in a variety of venues and she can be found on Twitter at @premeesaurus and on her website at http://premeemohamed.com.

About the Press

Neon Hemlock Press is an emerging purveyor of zines, queer chapbooks and speculative fiction. Learn more about us at www.neonhemlock.com and on Twitter at @neonhemlock.